Blessings always
Guruji

OM SHRI GANESHAYE NAMAH

the stories of braj

NAINA ASIJA

BlueRose ONE.com
Stories Matter
NewDelhi • London

BLUEROSE PUBLISHERS
India | U.K.

BlueRose ONE.com
Stories Matter
NewDelhi • London

For permissions requests or inquiries regarding this publication, please contact:

BLUEROSE PUBLISHERS
www.BlueRoseONE.com
info@bluerosepublishers.com
+91 8882 898 898
+4407342408967

ISBN: 978-93-93386-05-2

Cover Design: Muskan Sachdeva
Typesetting: Pooja Sharma
Cover Illustration by: Naina Asija

First Edition: February 2024

Acknowledgement

RADHE RADHE ! I dedicate this book, in gratitude to my Almighty Guruji Maharaj whose grace removed my illusions and helped me sail through on a journey that leads to eternal love.

AND

I also dedicate this book to my parents Late Shri Om Prakash Mehta and Shrimati Rani Mehta for their unconditional love, support and blessings.

Preface

'THE STORIES OF BRAJ' is a collection of short stories from the life of Lord Krishn during the tenure he spent in Braj. The land of Braj is highly revered by the devotees of Lord Krishn, as the Divine himself was born here and displayed his childhood pastimes until the age of eleven years.

All the stories are descriptive and are further enhanced by the colourful illustrations in water colours. The illustrations capture the essence of the moment being described in the story.

The following stories are written from the perspective of devotees who have voluntarily taken up the form of either a cow, a flower, a rock or a participant in the Krishn Leela in real-time. The reader will have a glimpse of deep love and adulation, which the devotees have for their Lord Krishn.

In fact, these souls strive to please the Divine Couple, and in response Sri RadhaKrishn magnifies the bliss many times over and return it back to the devotees.

My main inspiration for etching out these stories lies in listening to scriptures like, 'The Bhagavad Gita' and 'The Srimad Bhagavatam' from bonafied sources, throughout my formative years.

In Bhagavad Gita Shri Krishn says,

"ये यथा मां प्रपद्यन्ते तांस्तथैव भजाम्यहम्।"

"Ye yathā māṃ prapadyante tāṃstathaiva bhajāmyaham."

"I reciprocate the feelings and intensity of love of My devotees."

I was always fascinated and felt engulfed by the paintings, mosaics and sculptures depicting the stories of Krishn, that I would stand stunned while observing them. I was overwhelmed by what the artist was telling silently with every stroke of his brush, the colours he used and the patterns he made in his creation. To me each painting spoke volumes about the era gone by. 'The Stories of Braj' also has its roots in my visits and experiences I have had in Vrindavan, which lies in the state of Uttar Pradesh in the Northern part of India.

It all started when once, I had painted a scene from the Hindu epic Ramayan about Ahalya's liberation. On seeing the painting my son Divij enquired, as to what that painting was about, at which I first wondered, can't he see that this was one of the iconic scenes depicted from Ramayan. But on understanding that he was unaware of that subject, I then narrated him the story, of how Lord Ram's grace liberated mother Ahalya from the curse given by her husband Maharishi Gautam, of turning her into a stone and thus remaining invisible to the world and so on and so forth. It was at that moment, I realised that with every painting I painted I had to write the story explaining it as well.

I hope each one of you, who comes across this book is touched by the transcendental love of Sri RadhaKrishn.

Naina Asija

Contents

Introduction To The Land Of Braj

Braj is the absolute innermost chamber of the transcendent and eternal Golok Dham, which is the abode of Lord Krishn. Lord Krishn incarnated on Earth along with his abode, the Govardhan hill, Yamuna river and his confidential associates, with the help of his inconceivable potency Yogmaya Devi.

When Lord Krishn is pleased with our sincerity, the holy Braj Dham will be revealed to us. This forest is not just a sacred place but is Lord Krishn's playground for his glorious pastimes with his pleasure giving potency, Sri Radha Rani Ji.

Braj bhoomi is enchanting and is an embodiment of three divine opulances of being imperishable, free from sorrow and free from all types of fears.

"At Braj the Supreme Personality Lord Krishn, the object of Vedas, sweetly plays flute and protects the roaming cows, who have many good qualities and beautiful horns"- Rig Ved.

Shrimad Bhagavatam (BG16.44) gives a deeply moving description of Braj."How pious are the tracts of land in Vraj, for there the Primaeval Personality of Godhead, disguising himself with human traits, wanders about enchanting his many pastimes! Adorned with wonderfully variegated forest garlands. He is, whose feet are worshipped by Shiv ji and the Goddess Rama. He vibrates his flute, as he tends his cows in the company of Balram."

Braj, the land of Krishn is like an ocean, Mathura is like the lotus and Vrindavan is like the nectar pollen. All the residents of Braj, the Brijwasi are like flowers and Krishn is the bumble bee. Krishn is so tied by the bond of love with all the Brijwasi that, he remains eternally in spirit in Braj.

Braj bhoomi is made up of twelve beautiful sacred forests and several other sub-forests with river Yamuna meandering through the entire land through its course.

Some of the trees in Braj are ancient, out of which a few were planted by Sri Radha Rani ji herself about 5500 years ago. Devotees come and embrace them and place a desire before them.

The Braj bhoomi is full of Kunds. It is said that there are more than 250 Kunds in Braj bhoomi and each kund has a story associated with Lord Krishn.

Lord Krishn spent his entire childhood and adolescence under the care of his foster parents Nand Maharaj and Yashoda ji and amidst Gope Gwal, Gopis and cows. By the touch of Krishn's lotus feet, the land of Braj has become virtuous and successful.

Sri Radharani Ji's grace is beyond words. As soon as Sri Radha Rani hears the cry of her own people, forgetting her beloved Shyam Sunder, she immediately runs to them. It's only by her grace can one experience the topmost bliss (Braj Ras) of Vrindavan. She loves all the humble souls without any reason or cause.

It is believed that everything in Braj is conscious, be it the deities, their clothes, their ornaments etc.. All the places in Braj and the Leela Stalis are expanded for Nitya Leela to happen which cannot be seen by the naked eyes. Only by the grace of Shri Radha Rani ji, can one enter Braj and listen to the glorious pastimes of Sri Radha and Sri Krishn.

The land of Braj is alive with the Leelas of Shri Radha Krishn and the Gopis, which are believed to be still going on at a divine vibrational level. In their loving pastimes Shri Radharani Ji and Sri

Krishn are ever young. Though Priya and Priyatam always stay together but still, each time when they meet, it looks as if they have never met earlier.

Sri Radha Rani ji resides in everyone's heart in Braj. For everyone else Krishn is the Supreme but in Braj, Sri Radha Rani ji is the Queen who is celebrated as Vrindavaneshwari.

In Braj, it is believed that application of Braj Raj, listening and meditating on 'The Bhagvad Katha' and partaking Parikrama helps the soul to get liberated from the cycle of birth and death and thence, is eternally harboured in service of the lotus feet of Sri Radha-Krishn.

The present day Braj bhoomi was resurrected by passionate devotion of Sri Chaitanya Mahaprabhu and Vallabhacharya in the sixteenth century.

1

Lord Krishn

"Lord Krishn is playing the flute. His complexion is dark, like that of dense clouds just before rain. He is standing in a way, that his neck, waist and his feet are bent."

LORD KRISHN

"Shri Krishn is the primaeval Lord who is proficient in playing on his flute, with beautiful eyes like lotus petals, with head decked with peacock feather, with the figure of beauty tinged with hue of blue clouds and unique loveliness charming billions of cupids."

(Ref-Brahma Samhita by Srila Bhaktisiddhanta Saraswati Goswami Thakur).

Krishn is the supreme Lord, the source of all sources and who is present in every atomic and subatomic particle that exists. It is his life force energy that breathes life into our ecological system and sustains universal existence. He has given everyone the free will, so all the karmic results one gets in one's lifetime are self created by one's own thoughts, intentions and actions.

Lord Krishn comes to the planet earth to deliver the pious, annihilate miscreants and reestablish principles of religion. All his devotees are very dear to him therefore, he reciprocates to their love. Only a few people by his divine grace can recognize him in person when he incarnates and rest everyone's consciousness is clouded by illusion, so cannot understand or see the truth as it is.

During the battle of Mahabharat between Pandav and Kaurav, Lord Krishn spoke 'The Bhagavad Gita' to his dear friend Arjun and removed all his fears and illusions. The Bhagavad Gita is considered the ultimate guide book in Hindu philosophy, for all the answers one may be seeking in one's lifetime. Lord Krishn spoke about the importance of following one's duties, 'karm', the path that leads to liberation, about the universes that co-exist, his spiritual abode and declared Himself as the Supreme Personality of Godhead.

Lord Krishn said that, "Men of small intelligence worship the demigods and their fruits are limited and temporary. Those who worship the demigods go to the planets of the demigods but My devotees ultimately reach My supreme planet."(BG 7.23)

The Maha Mantra,

Hare Krishn Hare Krishn

Krishn Krishn Hare Hare

Hare Ram Hare Ram

Ram Ram Hare Hare

Was given by Lord Chaitanya Mahaprabhu. Chanting of this Maha Mantra and meditating on the words spoken by Lord Krishn helps the bonded soul to evolve in Krishn consciousness.

2

Janmashtami

JANAMASHTAMI

"As Lord Narayan appeared in the prison house of Mathura, the shackles of Vasudev and Devki opened and fell off on their own."

JANMASHTAMI

The blessed day has come when the entire universe is rejoicing. The demigods have arrived in Braj and are showering their blessing on all the five elements: air, water, fire, earth and ether. Due to which there is a surge of happiness, peace, prosperity and abundance in all directions. Also, in all the towns, villages and pasturing grounds of Braj there are signs of good fortune seen.

Auspicious stars are visible in the sky. The clouds are roaring aloud with thunderstorms and rain is filling the river bed of Yamuna river. The lakes are beautifully decorated with lotuses and the wind is blowing very pleasantly, carrying the fragrance of different flowers all over Braj.

The birds are singing and the whole forest echoes their sweet sounds. The peacocks with their open feathers are dancing with their consorts.

The sages are in bliss too, as all of a sudden they found their homes very pleasant to ignite the sacrificial fire. Due to the disturbances created by the demoniac King Kans, the sacrificial fire had been almost stopped in the houses of brahmins and sages. Being forbidden to offer sacrifices, they were very distressed in mind, intelligence and activities.

Anyhow, just at the moment of Shri Krishn appearance, automatically their minds became full of joy. They could hear loud vibrations in the sky, coming from transcendental sounds of trumpets, proclaiming the appearance of the Supreme Personality of Godhead, Lord Krishn.

It was the eighth day of the waning moon at midnight, in the month of Bhadrapad, the moon rose together with the star Rohini, when a bright golden light descended in a prison house of Mathura. Immediately then the shackles of Devki ji and Vasudev ji broke and fell off on their own. The gatekeepers fell unconscious and the locks of all the prison gates opened automatically. In just that moment, Lord Narayan appeared in his full glory. In the presence of his bright golden aura, darkness disappeared. In his four hands he held a club, a disc, a conch and a lotus flower. He was wearing yellow garments shining like lightning and shark shaped earrings which were swinging to and fro.

In his Divine presence, Devki and Vasudev were spellbound and fell on their knees. Lord Narayan, with his magnificent golden aura uttered, that in previous lives they had done a lot of austerities to have a son like him. But no one is like him in the entire cosmos, so he himself has appeared to be their son.

Lord Narayan instructed Vasudev ji, that as soon as he takes up the form of a baby, he must immediately leave the prison house and go to Nand Maharaj ji's house in Gokul, where he has to leave him and get back Nand baba's newly born daughter, to hand it over to King Kans, showing her as his own eighth child.

Devki ji requests Lord Narayan to take the form of an ordinary baby with two hands so that, she can experience the bliss of being a mother.

Lord Narayan turns into baby Krishn. Ecstatic mother Devki loves him a lot but due to fear of Kans, Vasudev ji very hastily places the baby in a basket and leaves for Gokul, keeping the basket on his head.

Leaving the prison undisturbed, he came out in the open where it was heavily raining. Walking barefoot and balancing baby Krishn on his head, he reaches the Yamuna river. To reach Gokul, Vasudev ji had to cross the river. He entered the river, but with every step he took forward, the level of the river kept increasing from the knees, to waist and then to the shoulders.

When Yamuna river was almost about to cover the face of Vasudev ji, then baby Krishn took his feet out of the basket. Touching Krishn's Divine lotus feet, Yamuna river receded and parted itself to give way to Vasudev ji.

Vasudev ji reached Nand Maharaj ji's house, where everyone was asleep. He placed baby Krishn beside Yashoda Mata and took her newly born daughter along and came back to Mathura. As he returned to the prison house, both Vasudev and Devki got shackled and all the gates got locked once again on their own. The gatekeepers also rose to consciousness.

In the morning, in Gokul, as baby Krishn cried in his loudest voice, everyone woke up. Sunanda and Nanda, sisters of Nand Maharaj, who were sleeping beside Yashoda mata, on seeing Krishn in utter delight, just ran outside and announced, "Nand ke Anand Bhayo" i.e, "Nand baba is blessed with a bundle of joy."

Janmashtami ('janam' means birth and 'ashtami' means eighth day) which marks the birth of Lord Krishn. It is celebrated every year till date.

3

Namkaran Sanskar

"Gargacharya Rishi is naming Rohini's son-Balram and Yashoda Ji's son-Krishn. Nand baba is sitting at the back and is very happy."

NAMKARAN SANSKAR

Nandbaba was a cowherd and he used to graze cattle in Gokul which was spread in 84 Kos (One Kos is approximately 2 miles). Nandbaba, being an expert cowherd, became the leader of all the cowherds. In those times, one cowherd had thousands of cows. Cowherds used to dwell where water and grass was easily available. On the banks of River Yamuna, there was a huge jungle and Gokul was in this jungle.

Nandbaba had a Kshatriya friend named Vasudev. They were best of friends. When the atrocities of Kans rose out of control, Vasudev along with his wife Rohini sent all his other queens to Nandbaba's place.

Kans, the king of Mathura, had imprisoned his cousin sister Devki along with her husband Vasudev, for he was scared of the oracle that foretold that their eighth son would kill him. Kans brutally murdered Vasudev's and Devki's newly born first six sons by smashing their heads on a stone wall, as he didn't want to take any chances of leaving any of their sons alive, which could become a threat to his life in future.

Devki's seventh pregnancy was portrayed as a miscarriage in front of King Kans, whereas the foetus was transferred from Devki's womb to Rohini's womb by Yogmaya Devi. The baby in Rohini's womb was Balram and was born at Nandbaba's place.

Vasudev ji's eighth son Krishn also was taken to Nandbaba's house immediately after his birth. Vasudev ji himself had gone to Gokul and left him in care of Nand baba and took his wife Yashoda mata's newly born daughter, when everyone was asleep, back into the prison house in Mathura.

The daughter born to Yashoda was Mahamaya herself, who had taken birth there by the instructions of Lord Narayan.

This way Nandbaba was a fatherly figure to Balram and Krishn. He raised them and took good care of them.

Later, Vasudev ji requested Saint Gargacharya to go and perform Namkaran sanskar, which is the naming ceremony, for both his seventh and eighth son, who were under the protection of his dear friend Nand baba at Gokul.

Gargacharya went there and met Nand baba and told his sole purpose for which he had come. He asked him to keep the ceremony arrangements very simple and at a place away from the public eye, so that evil Kans don't come to know about it or else, his own life would be in danger.

Gargacharya kept Rohini's son's name RAM but as he had a lot of strength so he was called BALARAM. Here Bal' means strength. He kept Yashoda's son's name KRISHN, which means the one who has dark complexion and who attracts all sentient beings. Gargacharya also predicted the greatness of both the children to their parents. He told them, 'they have come to remove tyrants and re-establish dharm'. Lord Krishn was hundred days old at his naam sanskar ceremony.

After completing the rituals, Nand baba gratified saint Gargacharya with food and gave him dakshina.

4

Makhan Chor

"Lord Krishn has reached the clay pot containing butter, forming a human pyramid."

MAKHAN CHOR

Lord Krishn was called 'Makhan Chor' which means the one who steals butter, though very lovingly by the damsels of Gokul. Mother Yashoda told the gopis in the village to tie their handis' in which butter was stored at a height, so Krishn couldn't reach it.

When no one was around, Lord Krishn would still sneak into the houses of gopis to steal butter. He would form a human pyramid with the help of his Sakhas and would reach the handis no matter how high it was hung. He would then break the handi, relish the butter, share it amongst his friends and further distribute it to the monkeys as well.

This beautiful leela of Lord Krishn gave immense pleasure to all the Brijwasi. Outwardly they showed anger and even complained to mother Yashoda for her son's mischief, but internally they were all beaming with great joy.

Even if for a few days, Lord Krishn didn't show up at their homes, they would start missing him and would go to mother Yashoda's house with some or the other kind of reason, but actually they would only go there to get soul soothing darshans of Lord Krishn.

5

Gopeshwar Mahadev

GOPESWAR MAHADEV

"Shiv ji also called Neelkanth Mahadev disguised himself as a Gopi to enter Raslila. Radha, Krishn and all Gopis are spellbound to see Shiv ji in such attire."

GOPESHWAR MAHADEV

Shiv ji while meditating on Mount Kailash was mesmerised with the Divine music coming from Krishn's flute. So he immediately left for Vrindavan along with his wife Parvati ji.

Reaching there, he moved towards Raas-sthali near Banshivat, from where the music was supposed to be coming. Mother Parvati was allowed to enter Raas-sthali but Mahadev ji was stopped at the entrance by Shree Lalita ji, as she was instructed by Sri Radha Rani ji, to let only gopis and Lord Krishn in, for the Raas Leela.

Lalita ji said,"Only if you become a gopi I shall let you in," to which Mahadev ji agreed. So she aided Mahadev with the clothes the gopis wear, ornaments and a veil to cover his face, so that no one recognizes him inside. She then gave him a Yugal mantra as a password and made him enter the Raas Sthali.

Lord Krishn came to know about Mahadev ji's presence there and then, therefore thought of playing a trick with him. He very lethargically said to the Gopis that,"I am too tired of dancing and playing my flute." Further, he rested under the Banshi Vat and stated, "Gopis I will now look at your faces one by one and so all of you stand in a queue."

Mahadev ji, who wasn't able to mingle with the Gopis uptill now, just stumbled upon his own ghagra'. Krishn chuckled and in sheer naughtiness said, "I will start with the gopi who is standing in front." Listening to which Mahadev ji ran and stood last in the queue, thinking that Lord Krishn would get too tired of seeing all the faces till he reached him, as there were thousands of them.

When all the gopis were queued up, Lord Krishn declared that,"I have changed my mind, so now I will start seeing faces from the one who is standing last in the queue."

Listening to this Mahadev ji's heartbeat grew faster than ever and out of agitation, he just rushed to stand in the front of the queue. Observing all this, Lord Krishn felt ecstatic. As he was enjoying this Leela, so to prolong it further, he hid his inner delight and instead portrayed sarcasm and said aloud,"I have spotted someone, who is shying away and rushing back and forth. I think she doesn't want to show her face, so now I want to see who this Gopi is?"

All the Gopis' attention got diverted from Sri Krishn towards this Gopi and wondered who this tall and hefty Gopi is? Then Lord Krishn hastily ran towards her, grabbed her wrists and removed the veil from her face.

Seeing Shiv ji in Gopi's disguise, Lord Krishn exclaimed in amazement,"Come Gopeshwar Mahadev, come." Acknowledging the presence of Mahadev ji among them and that too disguised as a Gopi, made the raas-sthali echo with chatter and riots of laughter. The whole vibe of the place changed for the better. It was then followed by a dance, by the duo Natvar (Krishn) and Natraaj (Shiv) which mesmerised everyone.

There is a Gopeshwar Mahadev temple in Vrindavan, where Shiv ji is dressed as a gopi and Shiv aarti is sung every evening.

6

Damodar Leela

DAMODAR LEELA

"At Nand baba's courtyard, Yashoda Mata is tying 3 Years and 2 months old Lord Krishn to a wooden grinding mortar. In the background the twin Yamla-Arjun trees can also be seen."

DAMODAR LEELA

Nand baba and mother Yashoda had nine lakh cows of their own and also they had distributed many cows on the birth of their son Lord Krishn as gifts. However, even after having so much cow's milk and its by-product at home, Lord Krishn would still steal butter from the houses of gopis. Then these damsels of Braj would come to mother Yashoda and complain about her lad, which really embarrassed her.

One day, after such complaints and seeing her son's face smeared with butter which he had eaten elsewhere, mother Yashoda got very angry and thought of punishing him. She got a rope and tried to tie Krishn with a wooden grinding mortar. But, every time she tried to tie Krishn, the rope would fall short by an inch. The mother tried tying him again by knotting another rope to the previous one, to make it longer but she would fail to tie her loving son, as the rope would fall short by an inch or two again and again.

After repeating this process several times, all her effort went in vain. Tired mother Yashoda got one more rope, and tried to tie Lord Krishn one last time and finally managed to tie him up. Lord Krishn kept weeping and said,"Maiya mori mei nahin makhan khayo" ("O mother I haven't eaten any butter").

As the story unfolds, a devotee asks a saint,"how did the creator of the cosmos get tied up?" To which the saint replied, the rope with which Lord Krishn got tied came from Radha Rani ji. It's only by the grace of Sri Radha Rani ji that, Lord Krishn can be tied and be available to his devotees.

Though this Leela takes place only between mother Yashoda and Lord Krishn, it is not called Yashoda Krishn Leela but instead it is called Radha Damodar Leela, as Lord Krishn got tied by the grace of Sri Radha Rani ji. There is a temple in Shri Vrindavan Dham called Sri Radha Damodar temple dedicated to this Leela where Lord Krishn and Radha Rani ji are worshipped.

Lord Krishn got his name 'Damodar' from this Leela, where 'dammu' means rope and 'udra' means stomach. As per vedic lunar calendar, the Damodar Leela took place in 'Kartik maas' so this month is also called 'Damodar maas'.

While being tied to the mortar, Krishn started to move around. His mortar got stuck between twin Yamla-Arjun trees in his house premises. As Lord Krishn pulled himself out from in between the trunk of the two trees, both the trees got rooted out, and fell off the ground. From the trees two demigods appeared. They first thanked Lord Krishn, for he had liberated them and then introduced themselves as sons of Kuvera, Manigriv and Nalkuvara. These demigods were cursed by Narad Muni ji as they were so intoxicated that they did not cover their bodies in his presence. They were cursed to take the form of twin Yamla-Arjun trees in Gokul and on pleas for mercy by them, Narad Muni said that they would be liberated by the Supreme Personality of Godhead himself. This prophecy of Narad Muni came true during this Damodar Leela.

'Ukhal Bandhan Ashram' is the holy site where the Damodar Leela of Lord Krishn had taken place.This ashram is situated within Gokul (or specifically old Gokul). It was once part of Nand Maharaj's courtyard. There is an old grinding mortar that is worshipped in this temple. The priest claims the grinding mortar to be there from five thousand years, when mother Yashoda had tied little Krishn to it. A grinding mortar is commonly referred to as 'Ukhal' in Hindi. The Damodar Leela is also called 'Ukhal Bandhan Leela' as Krishn was tied to Ukhal. Ukhal Bandhan Ashram is situated within Mahavan, the eighth sacred forest of Braj Mandal.

7

Gopis Of Vrindavan

GOPIS OF VRINDAVAN

"All the Gopis though seemingly engrossed in their daily chores like bringing water from the river Yamuna, milking, grinding spices, cooking, making garlands etc- but internally their mind is absolutely focused only upon Lord Krishn."

GOPIS OF VRINDAVAN

The cowherd girls of Braj are called the Gopis. They loved Lord Krishn intensely and wholeheartedly. While being involved in their daily chores like milking, getting water from the well, making garlands, churning curd, grinding spices, singing praises of the Lord etc. they always meditated on Shri Krishn and his pastimes.

When they went to complain to Yashoda ji about Shri Krishn stealing their butter, it was only out of love and were finding a reason to have a glimpse of her lovely son again.

They would peek from their house windows or from behind the trunk of the trees, when Lord Krishn would return home after grazing his cows from over the Govardhan hill.

When Lord Krishn used to play his flute, some of the gopis felt so ecstatic and started weeping. Some became so mesmerised, that they left their work undone and rushed to meet him. Some left the food on the clay stove, some just ran barefoot with their braids half done and some even left with kohl in one eye as they forgot to apply it in another eye. The gopis were in divine love and to be in devotional service to Lord Krishn was the reason they had taken birth.

During the rasa leela, to remove pride from gopis Lord Krishn disappeared. And so in deep sadness they sang a song which is known as 'Gopi Geet'. This song is considered as the heart of the epic Srimad Bhagavatam.

And when Akrur ji came to take Lord Krishn to Mathura, the gopis and gop-gwal lay themselves before the chariot to stop him from leaving Vrindavan. Such was their love for Krishn.

Later, when Lord Krishn became the king of Dwaraka he sends his best friend Uddhav ji, who had good knowledge of shastras and vedas to Vrindavan so that, on meeting the gopis he too experiences the highest form of devotional service and his heart too gets drenched in love for him.

The eight principal gopis who were most intimate friends of Lord Krishn and Radha Rani ji are Lalita ji, Vishakha ji, Indulekha ji, Chitra ji, Rangadevi ji, Sudevi ji, Tung Vidya ji and Champak Lata ji.

8

Prayer Of Braj Shila

BRAJ SHILA

"Lord Krishn always moved barefoot, till he was on the land of Braj. When he played his flute, it's sound made the rocks soften and so, the marks of lord Krishn's feet, his herding stick and cow's hooves got indented in rocks or shilas' "

PRAYERS OF BRAJ SHILA

Braj is a heavenly land. Anything associated with Lord Krishn becomes precious and worshipable here.

From the perspective of a Braj Shila comes a heartwarming prayer. Being a Braj Shila (rock) gives me immense pleasure. Lord Krishn used me to knock down the 'matkis' of Gopis, be it during the 'Makhan Chori Leela' or 'Khor Sankri Leela'. When Krishn ran over me I felt joyful but also felt worried for, if I was hot on any summer day, it might hurt my master as he always moves barefoot, blessing me and Braj Raj. Sri Krishn with so much love and insurmountable grace left his foot, stick and even his flute indentations upon me which are worshipable by his devotees, as I remind them of Krishn Leela.

Being a part of Lord Krishn's pastimes, I have so many stories to tell and share the nectarine bliss which I have experienced.

As a Braj Shila, I am revered by the devotees as You, my Lord Krishn, rested upon me during 'Go Charan'; played flute while sitting over me, listening to which my heart also melted just like any of the Gopis and the impression of your foot were indented upon me. Though all Shilas are of great significance in Braj but a few on which You left your marks are now worshipable. A few of which are scattered across Braj, I am mentioning below.

Shila at Shri Radha Damodar temple

In Vrindavan, there is a Braj Shila that has imprints of Lord Krishn's foot, his stick, his flute and cow's hoof. This Braj Shila is placed and preserved in Shri Radha Damodar temple of Vrindavan.

It is believed that, if one takes four circumambulations of this temple, it is equivalent to one Govardhan hill circumambulation.

Sindoori Shila on Govardhan

Another famous Shila is 'Sindoori Shila', about which it is said, once Shri Krishn told Radha Rani that, "There is no vermilion (Sindoor) on your forehead so your Shringar (adornment) is incomplete." On this Radha Rani said, "There will be a lot of delay in going to Barsana again and putting vermilion." Listening to which Shri Krishn said that, "You can get vermilion here on any rock of Govardhan by the friction of your finger." It was here on Sindoori Shila on the Govardhan hill, that Radha Rani ji rubbed her finger and vermilion powder appeared, which she put on her forehead. Even today, Vermilion appears in this Shila.

Phisalini Shila on Indrsen Parvat

There is a 'Phisalini Shila' which is on Indrsen Parvat, in Klapta village (कलापटा), KamyaVan approximately thirteen kilometres from Barsana. When the Gopas were tired after grazing their cows, they told Krishn that they can't walk any further. Then Krishn created a path on Phisalini Shila with his hand on which, when the Gopas sat they came sliding down effortlessly.

One can still pay obeisance to the Phisalini Shila and remember the beautiful pastimes of Sri Krishn, which took place more than five and a half thousand years ago.

Shila at Shyam Kuti

There is a place called Shyam Kuti which is a secret Leela Sthali of Shyam and Shyama. It comes in Govardhan parikrama way, near Sant Niwas. In it there is a very beautiful Ratan kund, the trees there are almost in a lying position as if doing dandvat pranam and a Shila is also well preserved there which has indentations of Radha Rani ji's foot. This place is very peaceful.

Charan Pahari in KamyaVan

In KamyaVan, on Indrsen Parvat is preserved an ancient Shila called 'Charan Pahari' which has indentations of Krishn's feet, his stick which he used while grazing his cows and the hooves of his Shyama cow. It is a highly revered place for the devotees of Sri Radha and Sri Krishn.

Charan Pahari in Nandgaon

There is one more Shila by the same name of 'Charan Pahari' which has foot impressions of Lord Krishn in Nandgaon.

Shila in Sankri Khor

There is a place called 'Sankri Khor' (सांकरी खोर) between Chikssoli Gaon and Barsana where on the Braj Shila (rock) one can see seven ancient symbols 1) Surbhi cow's hoof, 2) Kamdhenu's hoof, 3) Airavat elephant foot along with 4) Balram's and 5) Shesh Naag's impressions.

Then there is another Braj Shila in Sankhri Khor itself which has indentations of Sri Krishn's both hands, showing as if he lost balance while running down the Nav Vilasgarh hill. In Sankri Khor, the way is very narrow so at any given time only one Gopi could pass through. Krishn would stop these Gopis and ask for 'daan' (tax) for crossing the lane. Once the Gopis caught hold of Krishn when he had come to play Holi in Barsana. They dressed him like a Gopi, made him wear a 'jutti' (slipper), tied his hair in a 'choti' ('Choti Bandhan Leela') and asked him to give tax the same way as he would ask all the Gopis. Seeing this Leela, one of the Gopi felt compassion, after all he was just a child so loosened Krishn's hair which was tied in a tail. Krishn freed himself and while running down the hill, his foot slipped as he was wearing a jutti. Krishn always remained barefoot, till he remained in Braj. One can still have the darshan of 6) Krishn's jutti impressions and 7) his hands impressions where he loses his balance.

In the Sankri Khor itself there is a Shila, in which till date, the smell of fresh milk and curd comes. It is the spot where Krishn broke the matki of Chandravali Sakhi. Krishn would break Matkis of Gopis, when they refused to give 'daan' ('Matki Phod Lila'). Krishn along with his four friends Arjun, Subal, Madumangal and Labang used to ask for milk and butter as 'daan' from the Gopis coming from nearby sixteen villages. They would carry Matkis to give to Kans. Krishn stopped them with an intention that if King Kans's army was fed milk and butter, they would become stronger and the Brijwasi would become weak if they wouldn't be fed well therefore, could easily be defeated by Kans's army.

Shila on Indrsen parvat in KamyaVan in Adi Vrindavan

On Indrsen Parvat, Lord Krishn did his 'Go Charan' (गो चारण) Leela i e, he would take his cows for grazing from Nandgaon over to Indrsen Parvat, when he was five years old.

Once he was playing with his cowherd friends at Indrsen Parvat, when the Vyomasur demon disguised himself and started kidnapping his friends and taking them into his cave. Krishn killed the demon inside his cave.

To this date one can have a look at Vyomasur cave, in which his dead body still lies. Then on top of the hill one can have darshans' of the indentations of Krishn's right hand and right foot on a Shila, when he lost balance during the fight with Vyomasur. And just near to it, during the fight Krishn's 'Mor Mukut' (peacock feather crown) and 'Haar' (necklace) fell downhill whose impressions can still be seen.

Shyam Shila in Dabaara Gaon

This is a Shila on which Lord Krishn used to sit and play his flute. As Nand baba had nine lakh cows and the other cowherd friends of Krishn also got their cows there for grazing, so Krishn sat at Shyam Shila which is over a hill to overview lakhs of cows. When Krishn played his flute, the cows gathered near to the Shila and then they would together return back to Nandgaon at dusk.

The Shyam Shila is of the colour of Shyam himself i e, somewhat like the colour of dense black clouds just before rain. Other than this Shila, the rest of the rocks on the hill are of reddish hue.

Maan Shila in Mangarh, Gahvar Van

There is a Shila well preserved in the chamber of Maan Mandir which is on the peak of Mangarh range of Brahmanchal Parvat in Gahvar Van. It is that Shila on which Radha Rani ji sat upon when she was in 'Maan' (upset) with Lord Krishn. On the Shila the poojari puts six Tilaka, signifying the presence of Radha Rani on right side, Lord Krishn in gopi form on the left side of the Shila and four other Tilaks, two on each side signifying four Sakhis of Radha Rani ji. On the Maan Shila one can even see four lines representing braids, two each of Radha and Krishn. Lord Krishn had come dressed as a Shyama Gopi to decorate Radha Rani ji with flowers so that she gives up her 'Maan' and reconciles with him.

And on the side of this Shila, is another Shila, which is supposed to be Krishn's body as it is 'neelambar' (of blue colour as that of sky). One can even have darshan of one eye of Krishn in this Shila.

Khat Shila

Khat Shila (खाट शिला) is the rock on which Krishn used to take rest while the cattle grazed on the hills slopes. This rock has been blasted out and razed to the ground.

Saugandhini Shila

Saugandhini Shila is the rock on which Krishn vowed (सौगंध) to Brijwasi that he would never leave Braj.

Shila at Surya Kund

A Shila is preserved at Surya Kund, which has a clear impression of Radha Rani's Mukut (crown) which she used to keep on that Shila before entering the Kund to pray to the Sun God (Sury Dev).

Anjan Shila in Anjanokh, Barsana

Once on listening to the melodious notes coming from Krishn's flute, Sri Radha Rani ji, left hurriedly to meet her beloved Lord Krishn that she forgot to apply kajal in her eyes.

On seeing Radharani's eyes without Kajal, Lord Krishn rubbed his finger on Anjan Shila and Kajal came out which he applied himself in Radha Rani's eyes. One can still have darshan of this Shila at Anjan Bihari Temple at Anjanokh, Barsana. Here, on rubbing the Shila with a finger, kajal (Kohl) still comes out.

Bajni Shila in Mukhrai Gaon

Mukhrai is the village of Radha Rani's maternal grandmother Mukhara on whose name the village is named. She dearly loved her granddaughter and even after she was married in Javat Gaon, she used to go to see her everyday. As a child Sri Radha Rani Ji used to play with Bajni Shila, a rock which was hollow from inside and upon knocking at different ends, different sounds could be heard. This Shila is still preserved in one of the three temples of Mukhrai Gaon.

Shila in Shri Lalita Mandir, Uncha Gaon, Ator, Barsana

In Shri Lalita Mandir, there is an ancient Shila on which impressions of Lord Krishn, Radha Rani ji, Lalita ji and a cow are there, which are believed to be from Dwapar Yug, which was about five thousand five hundred years ago.

Chitr Shila or Phisalini Shila, Uncha Gaon, Sakhigiri Parvat, Barsana

In Uncha Gaon, on Sakhigiri Parvat, just under the Vivah Mandap of Lalita and Krishn is a Shila which is called 'Chitr Shila'. It is so named, as the marks of Mehndi of Lalita Ji's hands can still be seen there. This Shila is also called 'Phisalini Shila' as all the Sakhis of Radha Rani ji, when they were children used to slide on it.

Chitr-Vicitr Shila, Sakhigiri Parvat, Barsana

On the Sakhigiri Parvat, Barsana, on the way to a significant Krishn Leela spot 'Chappan Katore', one can have darshan of 'Chitr-Vicitr' Shila which has various marks of Mehndi (Henna).

Dandvati Shila, Govardhan

Dandvati Shila is believed to have been six feet tall when ShreeNathji left for Mewar. Due to the curse given by Pulastya muni to Giriraj Govardhan it reduces in size each day.This Dandvati Shila is already in the earth and so the land around it has been dug for darshan. It is believed, doing parikrama seven times around Dandvati Shila is equivalent to performing full Parikrama around Sri Giriraj ji.

9

Glories Of Braj Raj

GLORIES OF BRAJ RAJ

"Lord Krishn is sitting on the soil of Braj also called Braj raj'. He is sitting in the centre surrounded by all his Sakhas' who are joking and sharing their food with him. "

GLORIES OF BRAJ RAJ

The soil of Braj is locally called Braj raj. This holy soil is highly revered by the devotees of Shri Krishn. They pay their homage to the soil by 'dandvat pranam', 'namaskar', applying 'tilak' on their forehead and also by having granules of it. The most revered possessions of the saints of Vrindavan are Shri Krishn's darshan, Braj Raj and listening and meditating on everything that Shri Krishn said and did.

The Braj raj is eternal and has witnessed Divine pastimes. Lord Krishn moved barefoot on it, played, shared food and rolled over on this holy soil with his friends. Some of Krishn's close friends were Sridama, Subala, Arjuna, Gandharva, Vasanta, Madhu Mangal, Ujjavala, Kokila and Sanandna to name a few.

Go Charan Leela

Having risen early in the morning, Krishn blew his bugle made of horn and woke all the cowherd boys and calves with its beautiful sound. Then Krishn and the boys, keeping their respective groups of calves before them, proceeded from Brajabhumi to the forest.

Allured by green pastures, the cows would go grazing and Lord Krishn would then play with his Gopa friends. When Lord Krishn sat in the centre, encircled by his friends. he looked like the whorl of a lotus flower surrounded by its petals and leaves. He sat with his flute tucked between his waist and his tight cloth on one side and his horn bugle along with a cow-herding stick tucked on the other side of his waist. Every one of them was trying to look forward toward Krishn, thinking that Krishn might look toward him. They shared food, joked and laughed when having their lunch in the forest.

Virat Roop (Full Divine Form)

As a toddler, Shri Krishn was very fond of eating the Braj raj. When his elder brother Balram ji, who was also his best friend, tried to stop him but Krishn would not listen, so Balaram ji complained to mother Yashoda. And when mother Yashoda asked Krishn to open his mouth which was supposed to be full of Braj raj, but to her amazement inside his mouth she witnessed the whole sky, the planetary system, the luminaries in all directions, the sun, the moon, fire, air, the seas, islands, mountains, rivers, forests, and all kinds of moving and non-moving entities. This was baby Krishn's way of showing her mother that the whole cosmos is situated within him.

10

Prayers Of Flowers Of Braj

PRAYERS OF FLOWERS OF BRAJ

"Sri Radha Rani Ji and Lord Krishn are dancing and mother nature is rejoicing along. Lotuses are in full bloom in river Yamuna."

PRAYERS OF FLOWERS OF BRAJ

From the heart of every flower growing in Braj comes a prayer that, Oh! My Lord Krishn, we are immensely grateful to you, for being chosen to be sown in the land of Braj, coz' here we can constantly meditate at your lotus feet along with your devotees who are continuously engaged in providing service to you by making beautiful garlands.

Our life's purpose is complete when you adorn us on your headgear along with your peacock feather. We love to hang around in your neck as your garland and feel deeply privileged when we are kept under your lotus feet, where we can protect them from touching the hard ground beneath.

We feel extremely honoured when mother Radharani ji wears a flower crown, also called pushapara made either of yellow Jasmine, Ragini flowers, Navamalai flowers, Sumali flowers or gold Ketki flowers. Her floral crown enchants your mind and that's when our purpose of life is completed.

Your divine play with Radharani ji, in the scented Kadamba forest makes Radharani ji rejoice, sing and dance in ecstasy. Her happiness reverberates in nature and its repercussions starts showing up extensively, through splashing of colours by formation of rainbows, procreation, grassland start getting greener, forests denser, colours of flowers deeper and tastes of fruits sweeter.

Our mention in your leela is your grace. We are grateful that you loved adorning Gunja' flower mala and earrings made out of them as a child. Your Vaijayanti mala contains five different colours of forest flowers that reach down to your feet.

We are delighted as your eyes are compared to lotuses and feel extremely honoured when our petals are showered upon you.

During the Raslila on Sharad Purnima night, the flowers which were to bloom in another season (like Mallika, Kumud etc-) and the ones which bloom only during the day (lotuses) were in full bloom to serve you Lord Krishn.

11

Prayers Of Cows Of Vrindavan

PRAYERS OF COWS OF VIRNDAVAN

"All the cows are praying to Murli Manohar that they wish to quench their thirst from the river Yamuna and graze on the abundant glasslands of Braj, only if he plays his flute or Murli'."

PRAYERS OF COWS OF VRINDAVAN

The cows of Vrindavan are highly revered as Lord Krishn himself took them for grazing. From the perspective of cows comes a heartfelt prayer that, 'O' my master Sri Krishn, The Almighty one, please throw a loving glance at us, for only if you look at us can we graze from the abundant pastures of Vrindavan which are full of flowers and rich with nourishment for us.

'O' Murlidhar, just see how the blooming lotuses are attracting birds by their aroma. The humming of bees, cooing of cuckoos and cranes is echoing throughout the beautiful trees in the forest. Also, here the sands are clean and soft. Just see how this riverbank of Yamuna is extremely beautiful because of its pleasing atmosphere. For only if you glance at us can we really quench our thirst too.

Hey Murlimanohar, which thought of yours has captivated you for so long that you have even forgotten to play your flute, for you very well know we can only lactate when we listen to the melody you play.

Dear master, it is your causeless mercy and grace upon us that we have a respectable position across the Indian subcontinent.

Your names Govind and Gopal and your spiritual abode Golok and Gokul in Braj have a key reference to us. In Sanskrit language 'Go' refers to a cow, earth and senses. Lord Krishn, you are the giver of happiness to cows, earth and the senses and hence named Govind. You are the one who liberates everyone.

Lord you have blessed us in person by your gentle loving touch and by imprinting your muddy hands on our back.

When you were five years old you would take us for 'Gau Charan Leela' i.e, for grazing and over there when you felt thirsty, you would drink milk directly from the udder of Shyama cow. And as we grazed on the soft grass, you would play such melodious notes on your flute that we were completely mesmerised and would come running towards you.

The sound of your flute had a significant impact on the trees, which trembled in ecstacy and also on the rocks of Govardhan hill where we grazed. The rocks melted and the impression of Your lotus feet, along with your herding stick and our hooves got indented in the rock. These rocks or Shila are preserved and highly revered by your devotees.

In the book, 'Sri Radha-Krishn-Ganoddesa-dipika' written by Srila Rup Gosvami, mentions the names of some of Krishn's cows:- Mangala, Pingala, Pishangi, Manikastani, Hamsi, Vamsi Priya, Surbhi and her calf Manorath.

Kajari, Bahula, Kapila, Kanchana etc-, were also some of the cows who were very dear to you Krishn. You have also revealed that amongst cows you are Kamdhenu, the desire fulfilling cow.

12

Shri Shri Krishn Balaram

SHRI KRISHNA BALARAM

"Sri Krishn adorned in yellow clothes and peacock feather crown is holding his herding stick in one hand and has stretched his other hand around the shoulders of his elder brother Balram, who is wearing blue garments."

SRI SRI KRISHN BALRAM

Lord Balram has fair complexion and adorns blue clothes. He is the seventh son of Vasudev and Devki, but when in the womb, Lord Narayan intervened and instructed his external potency Mahamaya to transfer the embryo from Devki's womb into Rohini's womb. Thus, Shri Balaram was born from his surrogate mother Rohini, who is the first wife of Vasudev ji.

After Vasudev ji was freed from the prison by his both sons, Krishn and Balaram, Rohini gives birth to a daughter, Subhadra. So, Balram ji's younger sister is Subhadra and Lord Krishn being the eighth son of Vasudev and Devki is also the younger brother of Balaram ji. The mightiest of all Sri Balram was married to Kakudmi's daughter Revathi.

Balaram is an expansion of Lord Krishn and he is also one of His confidential associates who comes along when he plans to incarnate on planet Earth. In prior lifetime when Krishn incarnated as Lord RAM in Ayodhya, Balaram took birth as his younger brother Lakshman.

Shri Balaram is also called Sankarshan, Balabhadr and Halayudh. After Lord Krishn killed his wicked maternal uncle Kans, freed his parents Vasudev and Devki from prison and giving Ugrasen back his throne and making him the king of Mathura, both the brothers then went to study at Sandhipani Muni's ashram where in just sixty four days they mastered sixty four forms of arts. In Guru dakshina, Lord Krishn got back his Guru's son who had disappeared in the ocean in Prabhasa, near Dwarka. When on the search mission to get back his Guru's son, Krishn killed the probable demon Shankasur and obtained his conch Panchjany, which he later blew to announce the start and end of battle of Mahabharat.

When Krishn couldn't find his Guru's son Punardatta with Shankasur, then he went to Yamraj, the God of death and got his Guru's son back from him. There at the Sandipani Ashram Lord Krishn and Sudama also became close friends.

The demons killed by Shri Balaram in his childhood are:-

1. **Dhenukasur** - When Krishn and Balarama along with their friends went to eat the fruits in the palm forest also called Taal Van, the demon Dhenukasur attacked them in the form of a donkey. Balram caught his feet and swung him and threw him on the tallest palm tree, due to which he died.

2. **Pralambasur** - Once Shri Krishn was playing with Gopas and Balarama. At that time, Asur Pralamb also joined the friends and started playing a game. In the game the loser used to carry the winner on his shoulder. Pralambasur deliberately lost in this game and so Balaram sat on his shoulder. Taking advantage of this opportunity, he ran away with Balramji. Balaram increased the weight of his body so much that it became difficult for Pralambasur to escape. He could not even walk, so came back to his original form. There was a fight between Pralambasur and Balaram for some time and in the end Pralambasur was killed.

13

Govardhan Leela

GOVERDHAN LEELA

"On the advice of Lord Krishn, the Brijwasi' are giving their annual share to the Govardhan hill, which was priorly to be given to Indr Dev."

GOVARDHAN LEELA

The Brijwasis used to pay their homage to Indr, the rain God, by offering him food through yagn.

Observing all the preparations around Indr's worship, seven years old Lord Krishn stopped them from continuing this practice and instead asked them to pay their obeisances to the Govardhan hill in Vrindavan.

He said that the Govardhan hill is the King of mountains and through its abundant grasslands, crops and water bodies, it nourishes them and their livestock.

The surrendered Brijwasis offered everything which was originally prepared for Indr, to the Govardhan hill with great devotion and gratitude as instructed by Lord Krishn.

When Indr dev came to know that he did not get his annual share from the Brijwasi, he felt insulted, humiliated and thus became very furious. He then ordered the clouds to burst over Brajbhoomi and swipe off everything from there.

When torrential rains started pouring in Vrindavan, the Brijwasis ran to Lord Krishn and asked him to save them and their cattles from the wrath of Indr Dev. Lord Krishn told them, as of now the Govardhan hill is their saviour, so they should all go with their plea to him.

All Brijwasis along with their cattles ran towards Govardhan hill for protection. Lord Krishn lifted the mighty Govardhan mountain on his smallest finger of left hand and asked everyone to take shelter underneath it. Lord Krishn held the Govardhan hill for seven days and seven nights at a stretch. When the clouds with their all powerful thunderstorms and lightning couldn't destroy even a single tree from the Govardhan hill, they returned back and narrated the whole story to Indr.

Understanding then that Lord Krishn is the original Personality Of Godhead, Indr's pride was shattered and he accepted his defeat on the eighth day. He then approached Surabhi, the mother of all cows and a great devotee of Lord Krishn, to seek forgiveness from Krishn on his behalf. Lord Krishn forgave Indr and the Surbhi cow anointed Lord Krishn with her milk. Following that Surbhi declared Lord Krishn as 'Govind', which means the Lord of the cows. This is how that eighth day, which is called ashtami in Sanskrit, began being celebrated as Gopashtami.

All the Brajwasis were very glad and joyful as they were saved. To pay their obeisances, the Brijwasis prepared 'Chappan Bhog' (fifty six meals) for Lord Krishn as during his Govardhan Leela he had not eaten properly, his regular eight meals a day for continuous seven days, which equalled to fifty six meals in all.

Through this beautiful Govardhan Leela, Lord Krishn started being called 'Govardhandhari', which means the one who raised the Govardhan hill. Krishn himself had also declared that among mountains, he is the Govardhan.

To this date Govardhan puja is celebrated as Annakut puja on the fourth day after the festival of Diwali every year.

14

Gopi Vastraharan Leela

GOPI VASTRA HARAN LEELA

"Lord Krishn has taken all the clothes of Gopis and hid them on the Kadamb tree, when they were bathing in the river Yamuna."

GOPI VASTRA HARAN LEELA

All the gopis were sages who had incarnated in the Land of Braj to participate in the divine pastimes of Sri Krishn, to whom they were fully devoted and surrendered to.

There were some gopis who developed conjugal love for Lord Krishn and wished to have him as their husband. For their wish to come true, they prayed to Goddess Katyayani and observed fast for the whole month in order to please her and receive her blessings.

On the last day of their fast, early morning the gopis went to Shree Yamuna river to bathe, leaving all their clothes on its bank. Lord Krishn knew the intention of their fasting but before granting the fruit to their austerities, the Lord thought of teaching them a lesson on the code of conduct. As women they had created an offence of bathing naked in the river as there is the presence of Varun Dev ji in water.

Lord Krishn took away all the clothes of the gopis and hid himself. After a while, when the gopis came out to wear their clothes, they were taken aback, as there were none there. One of the gopis saw Lord Krishn hiding behind the canopy of a Kadamb tree. They all first frightened him and later requested him to return their clothes.

Lord Krishn told the gopis to come forth and collect their clothes from him. Divested of their robes, they came out of the Yamuna river. Thereafter, returning all their clothes Lord Krishn promised them that their wishes would be granted on forthcoming Sharad Purnima.

15

Gopi Geet

GOPI GEET

"During the Raslila when Lord Krishn disappeared, all the Gopis in deep agony were searching for their Lord Krishn. Some are asking the leaves and the creepers, some are searching behind the tree trunk and the bushes. Some are mimicking him, by playing a flute and some are trying to locate him through his footsteps."

GOPI GEET

It was Sharad Purnima night, when the gopis started sneaking out of their homes after listening to the musical notes coming from the flute of Lord Krishn, which he was playing in the Vrindavan forest.

When the gopis reached there, the Divine asked them to return back and be at their homes with their respective families at that hour. But the gopis persisted to be in his Divine's presence. Finally the Lord agreed to their request and allowed them to stay for that night.

While the gopis were strolling and having conversations with Krishn, they started having a sense of pride, thinking that they were the most fortunate women in the universe as the creator himself favours them. Feeling their sentiment of pride, Lord Krishn disappeared.

When the gopis couldn't see the Lord, they started searching for him. Some started following Lord Krishn's footprints, some looked behind the bushes and the tree trunks, some started asking the falling creepers and the leaves, as to where their Krishn was. Some in deep longing even started to mimic him and started to enact his various pastimes.

When their hearts were completely swollen with divine love and could hardly breathe, they started singing a song expressing their emotions. That song came to be known as Gopi Geet and listening to which Lord Krishn appeared again.

It is believed that even now at Nidhivan, in Vrindavan, the raslila takes place every night. The evergreen Tulsi trees of Nidhivan exist in pairs, out of which one is considered Gopi and the other one is considered Shri Krishn, who come to their original form and dance together every night.

16

Shree Radha Krishn Vihar Leela

SHREE RADHA KIRSHNA VIHAR LEELA

"During Raslila when Sri Radharani ji is tired of dancing and strolling around, then Lord Krishn picks her up in his arms as he walks in Vrindavan,"

SRI RADHA KRISHN VIHAR LEELA

During the Raas leela all the Gopis were so engaged in dancing with Krishn that each felt he was dancing only with her. All the gopis, except for Shree Radha Rani ji felt exalted and took pride in themselves of being in the company of Lord Krishn. Krishn gauged their emotions so disappeared along with Shree Radha Rani ji, as he dislikes pride in anyone and so wants to shatter it.

Radha and Krishn moved to a place in Vrindavan where flowers were abundant. There Lord Krishn adorned Radha Rani ji's braid with flowers and made her feel very special and loved. They then strolled for a while. Radha Rani ji asked Lord Krishn, if he could lift her in his arms as she was very tired of walking and dancing. Lord Krishn agreed happily and also took her for a boat ride on Yamuna river on that magical full moon night of Sharad Purnima. At that moment, Radha Rani ji felt very proud of herself thinking that she was very fortunate and most loved by the Lord as he chose to come only with her, leaving the rest of the gopis behind. Sensing an emotion of pride engulfing Radha Rani ji's mind, Lord Krishn left Radha Rani as well and disappeared.

Finding Lord Krishn nowhere Radharani started crying a lot. After some time the rest of the gopis too came there and asked Radha Rani ji as to what had happened. Shree Radha Rani ji then narrated the whole sequence of events to them and all of them together, seeked forgiveness and expressed their love for Krishn, by singing Gopi Geet. Listening to which Lord Krishn re-appeared and continued with the raslila.

17

Kali Kamli Wala

KALI KAMLI WALA

"Lord Krishn is wearing a black cloth around his neck which is referred to as 'Kali Kamli' in the local language of Braj."

KALI KAMLI WALA

Kali Kamli Wala is one of the popular names of Lord Krishn in the land of Braj. He is addressed by this name as he was often seen wearing a black cloth across his shoulders. The term 'Kali' means black and 'Kamli' means, blanket locally. The frightened mother Yashoda used to make Lord Krishn wear 'Kali kamli' a black cloth believing that this would protect her loving son from all evil eyes.

King Kans of Mathura would send demon after demon to Gokul for the purpose of killing his nephew Krishn. All the demons sent were either killed or tamed by Lord Krishn in very unique ways. Some of those demons sent by Kans were :-

In Gokul

1. Putana (a demoness)

Putna, a demoness who had taken up the form of a beautiful woman, tried to kill the six day old Krishn by feeding him with her poisoned breast milk. Krishn fed himself through her breasts but along with milk he squeezed life force also out of her body.

2. Sakatasur (Bullock cart demon)

When Sri Krishn was only three months old and was just trying to turn backside up, before he even attempted to crawl, mother Yasoda observed a ritualistic ceremony 'Kati- Parivartan' with her friends for the good fortune of the child. Such a ritualistic ceremony is generally performed with ladies who also have small children. When Krishn fell asleep, Mother Yashoda placed him in a cradle under a handcart so that he remained undisturbed and she went back and got busy with her household work pertaining to the auspicious ritualistic ceremony.

The Sakatasur demon who was looking for an opportunity to kill Krishn took shelter in the handcart. Anticipating the presence of a demon in the cart, baby Krishn, as usual for a child, began to kick his small legs. Baby Krishn then with the tip of his toe shattered the 'Shakat' which means bullock cart and thus the Saktasur who had entered in it the cart was killed.

3. Kagasur (Crow demon)

Kagasur reached near Krishn's cradle with the aim of gouging out the eyes of baby Krishn.

Kagasur was about to attack but Baal Krishn caught hold of him with his soft hands. Kagasur's condition became pitiable that he panicked, so fled off swiftly and fell down near Kans. He told Kans that some Mahabali had incarnated in Braj. Kans got scared and worried after hearing from him.

4. Trinavart (Tornado Demon)

Trinavart means tornado in Sanskrit language. Trinavart, the whirlwind demon, came to kill baby Krishn on his first birthday. He kidnapped him by taking the form of a tornado and took him higher up in the sky with an intention of killing him by throwing him down from a great height. But Krishn made himself so heavy that he couldn't bear his weight so the Trinavart demon hit the ground and was smashed to pieces.

Putana, Trinavart and Saktasur are the three demons whom Krishn has killed, who had come to the house of Krishn or to the courtyard at least. Putana came right into the house, Saktasur was in a cart outside his house, and when Trinavart came,Yasoda Mayi was sitting in the courtyard outside her house.

When Krishn was older, the demons attacked him when he went outside his house.

In Vrindavan

5. Bakasur (Crane demon विशाल बगुला पक्षी राक्षस)

Another time, when Krishn was tending the calves in the forest together with Balaram and the cowherd boys, the demon Bakasur came with the intention of killing Krishn. The Bakasur demon took the form of a bird. He looked like a huge crane (बगुला) with a giant beak. But Krishn seized this inimical demon by mouth and kept pushing his beak to a tree till it broke into pieces like a stick and then he tore his mouth apart and thus was mercilessly killed.

6. Aghasur (Python demon विशाल अजगर राक्षस)

Aghasur word is taken from Sanskrit language which means python. After Bakasur, Kans sent Aghasur, the older brother of Putana and Bakasur. This demon could not tolerate the transcendental pleasure being enjoyed in the forest by the cowherd boys and Krishn. He then assumed the form of a gigantic python. Aghasur opened his mouth with the intention of swallowing Krishn. His mouth was so big that the Gopas entered his mouth thinking it to be a cave. Seeing this Krishn also entered the python's mouth, but inside he expanded himself to an extent that Aghasur got suffocated and his body bursted.

7. Dhenukasur (Donkey demon गधा राक्षस)

Once the cowherd boys told Krishn and Balram that nearby is a very abundant forest, called Talavan which is filled with rows of palm trees. On the palm trees are grown sweet-smelling Tala' fruits which no one has ever tasted. Those Tala' fruits are now falling from the trees, and many are already lying on the ground, but as all the fruits are being guarded by the evil Dhenukasur, therefore no one can dare to enter the forest.

Listening to all this, Lord Balaram entered the Tala forest first. He with his arms began forcefully shaking the trees with the power of a maddened elephant, causing the tala fruits to fall to the ground.

Anticipating someone has entered the forest Dhenukasur, the ass demon rushed and fought with Balram. Balram held Dhenukasur's legs and wheeled him around which took his life and then he threw him on the top of the Taal tree (ताल, ताड़, palm). And when the dead demon landed on the treetop, the tree began to shake and with the weight of the demon fell off along with dead Dhenukasur.

Then together with Lord Balram, Krishn killed the ass demon and all his friends, thereby securing the safety of the Talavan forest, which abounded with fully ripened palm fruits.

8. Pralambasur

While Balram, Krishn and their cowherd friends were tending the cows in the Vrindavan forest, the demon Pralamb entered in the midst. He had assumed the form of a cowherd boy with the intention of kidnapping Krishn and Balram.

Balram struck the demon's head with his strong fist and dropped him dead.

9. Vatsasur (Calf demon बछड़ा राक्षस)

The demon disguised himself as a calf and intermingled with calves of Krishn. Krishn understood the intention of Vatsasur and grabbed him by his hind limbs. He swirled him so much that he lost his life out of dizziness and then Sri Krishn threw him on top of a tree.

10. Keshi (Horse demon घोड़ा राक्षस)

The demon who assumed the form of a gigantic horse was effortlessly slayed by Krishn by putting his hand in Keshi's mouth.

After seeing Keshi, Nand baba left Gokul and went to Nand Gaon with his family. After killing this demon Lord Krishn came to be known as Keshav.

11. Vyomasur (Bat चमगादड़ राक्षस)

On Govardhan hill, Krishn was playing a game of 'Stealing Lambs' with his cowherd friends. Therefore, some of the Gop-Gwal became lambs and some became thieves. Observing all this from afar, the Vyomasur demon, anticipating an opportunity to kill Krishn, participated in the game by disguising himself as a cowherd boy who was playing as a thief and stole many boys who were playing the parts of lambs. One after another he took away almost all the cowherd boys and put them in a cave on the mountain and sealed the mouth of the cave with stones. Krishn could understand the trick the demon was playing; therefore he caught hold of him exactly as a lion catches hold of a lamb. The demon tried to expand himself to escape arrest, but Krishn did not allow him to get out of his clutches. He was immediately thrown on the ground with great force and was killed, just as an animal is killed in the slaughterhouse.

12. Aristasur (Bull demon बैल राक्षस)

Aristasur demon entered Vrindavan in twilight. He was a bull with a gigantic body and a fearful appearance. Krishn caught his horns, broke them and thrashed him so much, as one washes clothes. He was so beaten up, that he died.

In Mathura

13. KUVALYPEERA (Elephant demon कुवलयपीड़ा)

In Marhura lord Krishn kills Kuvalypeera demon which shocks Kans.

14. Kans (King of Mathura कंस)

Even after sending so many demons, when Kans was unable to kill Krishn, he arranged for an 'Dhanush Yagya' in Mathura and sent Akrur ji to get Krishn and Balram so that he would kill them in Mathura itself.

In Mathura, Krishn confronts Chanur and Balram confronts Mushtik, both were the wrestlers of Kans. Krishn kills Chanur and as he sees Kans sitting unguarded he jumps towards him and dethrones him by bringing him down by pulling his hair. With a strong blow of his fist Krishn kills the evil Kans at once.

Krishn then frees his biological parents Vasudev and Devki from prison and makes Ugrasen, the father of Kans whom he had put behind the bars, the King of Mathura.

18

Swami Haridas

SWAMI HARIDAS JI

"Swami Haridas is playing a tanpura and singing Raag Malhar due to which it has started raining. Listening to his melodious songs, Sri Radha Rani Ji and Lord Krishn are so joyous that they appeared and are dancing in the rain."

SWAMI HARIDAS JI

Swami Haridas ji was a great devotee of both Lord Krishn and his consort Shree Radha Rani ji. He wrote poems in praise of the Lord and was a classical singer too. At a very young age, he renounced himself from all material attachments and went to Shri Vrindavan dham and engaged himself in service to Lord Krishn.

He is considered as an incarnation of Sri Lalita ji, one of the eighth principle gopis and an intimate friend of Sri Radhey. He meditated and sang at Nidhivan, in Vrindavan. It is said, when he sang Raag Malhar, a form of classical song in praise to Lord Krishn and Shree Radha Rani ji, it always rained.

His two disciples Baiju Bawra and Tansen were world renowned artists, of which Tansen was one of the nine gems in King Akbar's court.

Pleased with devotional service of Swami Haridas ji, Lord Krishn and Shree Radha Rani ji appeared in person and blessed him.

However, the beauty and charm of the divine couple was so much that the mortal beings (disciples of Haridas ji) were not able to bear it. Observing this, swami ji requested Shri Radhe-Krishn to take a unified form like Ghan (cloud) and Damini (lightning). Obliging the request of their devotee, Shri Shyama-Shyam merged into a single black charming idol of Banke Bihari ji.

Later Shri Banke Bihari idol was shifted from Nidhivan where he had appeared, to the Banke Bihari Temple where he resides even today. The temple is visited by thousands of devotees everyday.

Swami Shri Haridas made clearer the path to Nikunj Ras through complete surrender. He is considered to be the Adya Acharya (original Guru) propagating Madhurya Bhakti. However in Braj Mandal, Madhurya Bhakti as well as Prema Bhakti both are widely practised and are intermixed beyond recognition.

Swami Haridas ji's tomb is situated at Samadhi Mandir in Nidhivan.

19

Monkeys Of Vrindavan

MONKEYS OF VRINDAVAN

"Monkeys of Vrindavan, can be seen in Kunj Galis, snatching food stuffs from the visitors and hanging on the electricity pole wires."

MONKEYS OF VRINDAVAN

It is believed that one can go to Shree Vrindavan Dham only by the permission of the Queen of Vrindavan, Shree Radha Rani ji. When one enters Vrindavan one tends to listen to the sounds of temple bells and the pleasing chants of 'Radhe Radhe' all over. There the people chant 'Radhe Radhe' instead of having simple conversation. For example, whether one wants to ask someone, to give space to move forward or say thank you for the Prasadam' or for that matter, even greet someone, people chant 'Radhe Radhe' and the intention of their specific want is understood correctly.

While moving in the Kunj galis one cannot ignore the notorious monkeys there. One has to be very alert and careful with one's belongings, especially spectacles and also of eatables of all sorts, ranging from bananas, peanuts or even a packet of potato chips. The monkeys love it all and would find a way to snatch it from you no matter how guarded you may feel. And then, to get your belongings back one has to bribe them for something that they are ready to accept and barter for. Lately they are loving the Frooti juice for which they are ready to return the snatched goods.

Except on the trees, the monkeys can be seen everywhere else. They are in the Kunj galis (bylanes), on the temple walls and even hanging happily on electricity pole wires.

As the monkeys live in Vrindavan so the devotees love them too. They feed them well with Prasadam' and don't harm them at all and in fact, believe them to be the devotees of Shri Krishn too.

Shree Vrindavan Dham is mystical, magical and all its stories are full of surprises. Only the saints and devotees can understand the significance and the divine grace of Shri Krishn and Sri Radha Rani ji, for letting humans, animals and plants to reside happily in their abode.

20

Vrindavan Dham

VIRNDAVAN DHAM

"Lord Krishn and Sri Radha Rani Ji in their abode Golok, which is in the shape of a lotus flower. Everything that is below in the material realm is the reflection of what is above in the spiritual realm."

VRINDAVAN DHAM

When Lord Krishn appears on the planet Earth his confidential associates like Balaram ji, Shree Radha Rani ji, Narad Muni ji etc. and his Dham (abode) also descend with him. Lord Krishn's abode in the spiritual sky is called Golok Vrindavan and the replica of it descends on our planet, which is called Bhuma Vrindavan where Lord Krishn plays his childhood Leelas.

As heat and light are non different from sun, so in the similar way, Lord Krishn's name, form and abode are also non different from Lord Krishn. They are the same as Lord Krishn Himself.

The Mathura-Vrindavan area is called the Braj bhoomi which is of eighty four kos (one hundred and sixty eight miles). Vrindavan has got its name from a plant called Tulsi 'Holy Basil' (also called Vrinda devi), which grows profusely there. The Tulsi trees and also many other trees there are considered 'Kalpavriksh', who have voluntarily taken up the plant form to help Lord Krishn in his Divine play.

Lord Krishn is the most attractive one, as he attracts everything towards him. But Sri Radha Rani ji is the one who attracts and enchants Lord Krishn, so she is considered even greater and more powerful than Lord Krishn. The people in Vrindavan glorify Radha Rani ji by chanting her nectarean name 'Radhe Radhe' which is the complete form of Prem, Rasa and Anand. For many devotees Sri Radha Rani is the goal and for some, to be at the lotus feet of Sri Krishn is all that they thrive for. Brijwasis very well understand that, if Sri Radha Rani ji recommends their name to Lord Krishn, then he will accept them and their services.

21

Holi Utsav

HOLI UTSAV

"Sri Radha Rani Ji in pink garments has come to play Holi with her beloved Lord Krishn. The devotees are playing mridangam."

HOLI UTSAV

From the perspective of an observer to the delightful episode between Shyma-Shyam on the advent of Holi festival comes a playful vision, It is Holi today, the festival of colours and Shree Radha Rani ji is ready with gulal in all vibrant hues, a few rose petals and lots of water, coloured with dry palash flowers. Radharani ji is extremely happy and has worn light pink dress, so that she can later admire the colours she has got all over herself rubbed by her beloved Lord Krishn.

This is such a beautiful festival of love expression through colours. Mother Radha Rani ji is all set and dances her way through the Kunj galis along with her friends. The sound of her nupur, payal, bangles is reverberating all over the cosmos and the devotees match the beats of their mridangam to the celestial sounds of Radha Rani Ji's ornaments. Nature is desperately waiting to see the new colours that will be formed, when the Divine couple plays Holi.

"Oh see there Krishn has come!" Shree Radha Rani ji exclaimed with happiness. "Dear Sakhis, be fully prepared as we all have to colour the Creator and the Source of all sources completely with our love; Let him know that we love him and are grateful to him for engaging us in his esoteric pastimes."

When Lord Krishn approaches closer, all the gopis are spellbound by his majestic beauty. Seeing them stunned, Shree Radha Rani ji in playfulness, claps and reminds them to throw colours or else, they will lose in the game, of who is drenched first. It is almost like a battle between Nandgaon and Barsana (respective villages of Lord Krishn and Sri Radha Rani ji).

Redeeming their senses, all the gopis hastily along with Shree Radha Rani ji form a circle around Lord Krishn, shower rose petals and colour him completely with red, blue, green, yellow and purple colours.

TRIVIA

As per a legend, when Srimati Radha Rani was born, Mukhra Devi, Radha Rani Ji's maternal grandmother lit up the lamps on the chariot wheel and danced with it on her head. Later with passage of time, this dance came to be known as Charkula dance. It is believed that it comes from the word 'Chakra' which means wheel or a circular shape. It is still performed in the Mukhrai village on the last day of Braj Holi festivities.

Associates Of Radha And Krishn

Associates of Lord Vishnu who descend from Vaikunth do not actually fall. They come with the purpose of fulfilling the desire of the Lord, and their descent to this material world is comparable to that of the Lord. The Lord comes to this material world through the agency of his internal potency, and similarly, when a devotee or associate of the Lord descends to this material world, he does so through the action of the spiritual energy.

BALARAM - elder brother of Lord Krishn and son of Rohini and Vasudev. He is also called Sankarshan and Halayudh. He is known for his amazing strength and is often seen carrying a plough and a club. He wears blue garments. Sri Baldev is that personality from whom all bonafide spiritual masters manifest. He killed Dhenukasur, the ass demon. He, as a spiritual master, removes ass like ignorance from within the heart.

BRIJWASI - inhabitants of the land of Braj.

CAMPAKALATA - she is the third of the eight principal gopis. She is one day older than Radharani. Her complexion is the colour of blossoming yellow champaka flower.

CHITRA - she is the fourth of the eight principal gopis. She is twenty six days younger than Radharani ji. Her complexion resembles the colour of kunkuna and her garments are of the colour of crystal.

DEVKI - mother of Lord Krishn and wife of Vasudev ji.

GARGACHARYA - the reputed priest of the Yadu dynasty. He is credited with naming the eighth incarnation of Lord Vishnu i.e, Sri Krishn.

GAWAL - cowherd boys of 'Braj'.

GOPAL - Krishn was called by this name. It means cowherd where 'Go' means cow and 'Pala' means the one who protects.

GOPESWAR MAHADEV – Shiv Ji.

GOPI - the gopis are literally the cowherd ladies of Shri Braj Dham who are in total control of their senses, because they are totally absorbed in their love for Sri Krishn. They are never distracted by any other sentiment or desire.Their love for the beloved is uninterrupted and their one and only joy is Sri Krishn.

GOSWAMI - the six Goswamis who were disciples of Sri Chaitanya Mahaprabhu were asked by their Guru to produce a prolific amount of writings regarding Vaishnav philosophy and practices. They dedicated a significant amount of their time to uncover many ancient and sacred areas of land in Vrindavan associated with Sri Radharani ji, Sri Krishn and the Gopis. The six Goswami's were, Rup Goswami, Sanatan Goswami, Jiva Goswami, Gopal Bhatta Goswami, Raghunath Bhatta Goswami and Raghunath Das Goswami.

INDULEKHA - she is the sixth of the eight principal gopis. She is three days younger than Sri Radharani ji. Her complexion is tan and wears garments of colour of a pomegranate flower.

KAURAVAS - the hundred sons of Gandhari and Dhritarashtr, the Queen and the King of Hastinapur.

KUVER - the treasurer of demigods.

LALITHA - of the first of eight principal gopis. She is also the eldest of all gopis and is twenty seven days older than Radha Rani ji. She is famous for being the constant companion and follower of Sri

Radharani ji She is hot tempered by nature and her garments are like peacock feathers.

LORD KRISHN - He is identified by the vedic authorities as the source of all sources, of all that exists in the material and spiritual world.

MADHUSUDAN - Krishn who has nectar of gopis like bees.

MANIGREEVA - son of Kuvera.

MAHAMAYA - Mahamaya means the external potency of the Lord which puts a conditioned soul into the illusion that he will be happy by material adjustment. Mahamaya is Durga.

She is the superintending Goddess of this whole material world. Everything is going on under her control. Maya which drags a person from the Supreme Personality of Godhead is called Jadamaya (जड़ माया) or Mahamaya.

Mahamaya is the perverted reflection of Yogmaya. Nothing can exist in this cosmic manifestation that has no real counterpart in the spiritual field. All material manifestations are emanations of the Transcendence. The erotic principles of amorous love reflected in mixed material values are perverted reflections of the reality of spirit.

NALAKUVER - second son of Kuvera

NAND - Nand is the king of cowherd men of Gokul. His elder brothers are Upanand and Abhinand and his younger brothers are Sannand and Nandnan. He is an intimate friend of Maharaja Vasudeva and his wife Yashoda Maiya also has great friendship with Devki. Nand and Yashoda are parents of Sri Krishn, so Sri Krishn is also called NandNandan means son of Nand (Ref-Adi Puran). Nand baba's most intimate friend is Vrishbhanu ji.

NARAD MUNI - great sage and devotee of Lord Narayan.

NARAYAN - the four-handed incarnation of Lord Krishn.

NEELKANTH – Shiv ji consumed the poison that originated from the sea when Devas (Gods) and Asuras (Demons) churned the ocean in order to obtain Amrit. This poison that emanated during the Samudra Manthan (churning of the ocean) made his throat blue in color. Thus, Shiv ji is also known as Neelkanth, literally meaning The Blue Throated One.

PANDAVS - they were the five sons of Kunti and Pandu. Kunti and Krishn's real father Vasudev were siblings. Kunti's father gave her to his childless cousin Kuntibhoja. Also Lord Krishn's sister Subhadra was married to Arjun, one of the five Pandavas.

PARJANY - Lord Krishn's fair-complexioned, white-haired and white-attired grandfather is named Parjany Maharaja, because he is like a great cloud (Parjany) showering the nectar of auspiciousness. He is the best of all the residents of Vraj.

PARVATI - wife of Shiv ji.

RADHA RANI - beloved of Lord Krishn. She arranges for all souls to interact with Shri Krishn, without them being aware of His Supreme position. She is the Queen of Vrindavan and wears Ruby red upper garment, cloud blue lower garment and blue bangles. Her father is Vrishbhanu. and mother is Kirti Devi ji. Kirtid Devi is also known as Ratnagarbh Devi.

RANGADEVI - she is the seventh of eight varistha-gopis. She is seven days younger than Sri Radharani ji. Her complexion is of Lotus filament and her garments are of the colour of red rose.

ROHINI - wife of Vasudev who bearded her husband Vasudev ji's and Devki's child, Balaram in her womb with the help of illusionary potency of Lord Krishn i.e, Durga Devi or Mayadevi.

RUP GOSWAMI - one of the six main Goswami of Vrindavan. He is considered as incarnation of Rup Manjari, the most important of eight confidential maidservants of Sri Radharani ji. He has written several books.

SANDIPANI MUNI - Sandipani Muni was the Guru of Lord Krishn who lived in Awantipur. His wife was Sumukhi Devi. Sandipani's mother Pauranmasi Devi was an incarnation of Yogmaya Devi. She went to Gokul on the advice of her guru Devarsi Narad Muni. Sandipani's daughter was Nandimukhi devi and his son Punardatta who was rescued and returned to him, as Gurudakshina by his disciple Lord Krishn. His other son Madhumangla was a constant companion of Sri Krishn.

SHURSEN - father of Vasudev.

SUDEVI - she is eighth of most exalted gopis. She is the sister of Rangdevi and is sweet and charming. Her qualities are so similar to Rangadevi that they are mistaken for one another.

TUNGAVIDYA - she is one of eight principal gopis. She is hot tempered and wears white garments. She is an expert at dissimulation.

VASUDEV - father of Lord Krishn and the King of Vasu.

VRINDA DEVI - she has a beautiful complexion the colour of molten gold. She wears blue coloured garments. She is one of most important messenger gopi as she expertly knows the geography of Vrindavan. Her sister is Manjari. Vrindavan is named after her and she always remains there.

VRISHBHANU - he is the King of the cowherd folk of Barsana. He is the father of Sri Radha Rani Ji.

VISAKHA - she is the second most important of eight vrishtha- gopis. She was born at the exact same moment when Sri Radharani ji appeared in this world. Her garments are decorated with stars and her complexion is like lighting.

YAMUNA - Lord Krishn blessed and sanctified the river Yamuna. He did his boating pastime here.

YASHODA - Mother of Lord Krishn and wife of Nand Maharaj. She is the Queen of Vrajbhumi. She bestows(da) fame(Yash) to the inhabitants of Vraj hence named Yashoda. Yashoda Mata's closest friends are Kirti ji (the mother of Sri Radha Rani) and Devki ji, (the wife of Vasudev ji). She has two sisters Yasodevi and Yasasvini.

YOGMAYA - Yogamaya is the name of the internal potency that makes the Lord forget himself and become an object of love for his pure devotee in different transcendental mellows. This Yogamaya potency creates a spiritual sentiment in the minds of the damsels of Braj by which they think of Lord Krishn as their paramour. Any pastime conducted by the Supreme Personality of Godhead is an arrangement by Yogamaya not Mahamaya.

Yogamaya means the mercy of the Supreme Lord which connects a devotee in the transcendental loving service of the Lord. That is Sri Radharani ji.

Glossary

ACHARYA (आचार्य) - a spiritual preceptor, a founder or a leader of a sect, religious instructor

AKASHVANI (आकाशवाणी) - oracle

ASHTAMI (अष्टमी) - eighth day of Hindu lunar calendar

ATMA (आत्मा) - spirit

BAITHAK (बैठक) - an assembly site for recitation by a great Acharya

BAL LEELA (बाल लीला) - childhood pastimes

BANSHIVAT (बंशी वट) - holy place on the banks of river Yamuna where rasa leela took place. Banshi Vat is located on the Bank of river Yamuna on Parikrama Marg in Vrindavan and is near to Keshi Ghat. Here 'bansi' means flute and 'vat' means Banyan tree.

BHOG (भोग) - the food that will be offered to the deity. When offered it becomes Prasad' and then distributed

BHOOMI (भूमि) - land

BRAJ RAJ (ब्रज रज) - holy soil of Braj

CHOONA (चूना) - Calcium oxide (CaO) Explanation: Chuna is called Quicklime in english. The chemical name of Quick lime is Calcium oxide, having chemical formula CaO. Quicklime is used for whitewashing as it produces calcium hydroxide (CaOH) when it reacts with water.

CHOR (चोर) - thief

DAKSHINA (दक्षिणा) - dakshina is a Sanskrit term that refers to an offering or gift, typically to a Guru or priest

DANDVAT PRANAM (दंडवत् प्रणाम) - ritual offered by devotees to pay their respect to God, bow. In it the devotee falls like a stick (डंडा) at the feet of a deity or a Guru

DARSHAN (दर्शन) - an opportunity to see or an occasion of seeing a holy person or the image of a deity

DEV (देव) - demigod

DHAM (धाम) - eternal and divine abode

DHARM (धर्म) - the basic principle of divine law in Hinduism, Buddhism and Jainism; a code of proper conduct conforming to one's duty and nature

GEET (गीत) - song

GHAGRA (घाघरा) -) a long skirt, worn by women in South Asia

GHAT (घाट) - a series of steps leading down to a water body

GOKUL (गोकुल) - it is the place where Krishn spent his childhood

GOLOK (गोलोक) - it is a celestial abode of Sri Radha Rani ji and Sri Krishn

GOVARDHAN (गोवर्धन) - it is a hill in Vrindavan, which is appropriately named. Here 'Go' means cow and 'Vardhan' means nourishes, hence its grass nourishes Krishn's cows

GUNJA (गुंजा) - the bright red seeds of fig tree

HOMAGE - special honour or respect shown publicly

HOLI (होली) - hindu festival in which people throw coloured water on one another.

JANMA (जन्म) - birth

KADAM (कदम्ब) - *Neolamarckia cadamba*, with English common names burflower-tree, Leichhardt pine and called kadam locally, is an evergreen, tropical tree native to South and Southeast Asia

KALI (काली) - black colour

KATI PARIVARTAN (करवट बदलने का उत्सव) - when three months old baby Krishn was slanting his body to attempt to rise and turn around, this attempt was observed by a Vedic ceremony. In such a ceremony, called Utthana, which is performed when a child is due to leave the *house* for the first time, the child is properly bathed.

KALPAVRIKSH - desire fulfilling trees

KISHORI (किशोरी) - ever youthful, one who never ages

KOS (कोस) - is the Vedic measure of distance used in ancient India. One Kos is equal to approximately 168 miles or 2 to 3.5 km

KUND (कुंड) - pond, small reservoirs of water

KUNJ GALI (कुंज गली) - bylanes in Vrindavan

KARTIK (कार्तिक) - most dear month to Lord Krishn.

LEELA (लीला) - Divine act, play, pastimes

MAAN (मान) - a special stage in divine love in which the devotee develops so much love for God as to even attain the right of getting angry with Him. To do Maan means to sulk. When Radha Rani would not like anything about Krishn she would be upset (Maan) and then Krishn would try to rekindle their love by either fanning her, showing a mirror, and even serving her feet with humility

MAHABALI (महाबली) - One with great strength, A man of great strength, might and power

MAHARAJ (महाराज) - a great King or a ruler, a term for respect for brahmans

MAKHAN (माक्खन) - butter

MANDALA (मंडला) - circle, zone, circumference, a group

MURLI MANOHAR (मुरली मनोहर) - Sri Krishn was popularly called by this name too. It means he looks good with flute

NAMASKAR (नमस्कार) - the action of putting the inside of your hands together in front of your chest or face and bending your head forward when you meet somebody

NITYA (नित्य) - eternal

POORNIMA (पूर्णिमा) - full moon day

PRASAD (प्रसाद) - blessings (from deity)

PUSHAPARA (पुष्पारा) - these crowns of Radharani are made of flowers and buds of five different colours arranged in five points. Lalita Devi learned to make these from Sri Radha Rani ji

RAAS (रास) - this dance is part of the traditional story of Sri Krishn described in Hindu scriptures such as the Bhagavat Purana and literature such as the Gita Govinda, where Sri Krishn dances with Sri Radha Rani Ji and gopis

SAMADHI (समाधी) - cenotaph, a monument, sometimes in the form of a tomb to a person or group of persons buried elsewhere

SAROVAR (सरोवर) - a large lake or pond

SHARAD (शरद) - Winter

SHARAD POORNIMA (शरद पूर्णिमा) - a religious festival celebrated on the full moon day of the Hindu lunar month of Ashvin (September to October), marking the end of the monsoon season

SHASTR (शास्त्र) - (in Hinduism and some forms of Buddhism) a work of sacred scripture

SHILA (शिला) - a rock, a large piece of flat stone

STHAL (स्थल) - a site

TEERTH (तीर्थ) - sacred place

TILAK (तिलक)- in Hinduism, the tilaka is a mark worn on the forehead, sometimes other parts of the body such as neck, hand or chest with sandal and saffron

TULSI (तुलसी) - commonly known as holy basil. It is an aromatic perennial plant and is the most dear plant of Lord Krishn

USTAV (उत्सव) - festival

VAN (वन) - forest

VARISHT (वरिष्ठ) - principal, most important

VASTRA (वस्त्र) - clothes

VED (वेद) - any of the four collections forming the earliest body of Indian scripture, consisting of the Rig Ved, Saam Ved, Yajur Ved and Atharv Ved

VIHAR (विहार) - wandering, roaming or recreation

VIRAH (विरह) - agony of separation

WITNESS - observer

YAMUNA (यमुना) - river also called Kalindi

YUGAL (युगल) - Shri Radha and Krishn together

About The Author

Naina's primary interest since childhood has been in seeking The Truth, which led her to make choices like study sciences and scriptures. Being a textile designer by education, she has an eye for detail and her keen observation helps her in illustrations.

She is an avid traveller, a voracious reader and has an interest in subjects like sciences, autobiographies, wellness and mythology.

Her art of storytelling is simple, easy to understand but at same time very profound and takes the reader along in time. Her writing creates heart to heart connection and therefore the reader somewhere feels immersed, their soul stirred, immense joy, love and as a result, is mentally uplifted.

Her purpose of writing 'The Stories Of Braj' is to cultivate knowledge about Lord Krishn, awaken a transcendental desire of love and service for Lord Krishn. This book is like a drop in the vast ocean of unparalleled knowledge about our Indian history.

Naina Asija

THANK YOU